Books by Paige Sleuth

FROZEN
in CHERRY
HILLS

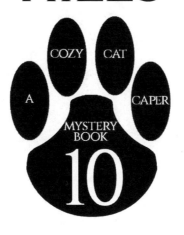

PAIGE SLEUTH

CHAPTER ONE

"It's a nasty habit, but I can't seem to stop," Maura O'Malley said to Katherine Harper, taking another puff from her cigarette.

Kat cinched her coat tighter, wishing she had thought to grab her mittens from her desk before heading outside. "I understand."

Maura blew out a breath, smoke swirling in front of her. Kat could see her own breath as well, but she blamed the cold for that. It was only the last day of November, not even winter yet, and it was already freezing. It didn't help that it had snowed all Thanksgiving weekend, the results of which now sat in heaps alongside the sides of their office building. Kat felt as if she'd been dropped into the middle of Siberia.

She needed a better coat, she decided. Either that or she would have to make sure she didn't volunteer to accompany Maura on any more of her cigarette breaks until the first spring blossoms made an appearance in Cherry Hills, Washington.

Kat eyed her new boss, who didn't seem bothered by the cold. Maura's cheeks were as rosy as they had been inside, although maybe that was the result of her wearing so much makeup. Kat suspected that with Maura's lush brown hair, green eyes, olive complexion, and wide smile she would be pretty even without the makeup.

Although, Kat couldn't help but think, Maura would be ten times more attractive if she'd lose the cigarette in her hand.

Maura toed a patch of snow. "This will sound crazy, but I feel like smoking is part of my identity. I mean, I started when I was twenty. That's over half my lifetime ago. How do you shake something that's been with you your entire adult life?"

Kat shifted from foot to foot in a vain attempt to get her blood circulating. "I hear it's a tough habit to break."

"It's the worst." Maura paused, then said, "Have you noticed not many people smoke in

Cherry Hills? Why do you think that is? Before I moved here I knew a bunch of smokers. We used to . . ."

Kat mentally willed Maura to stop talking and start working on getting her nicotine fix. As much as she liked her new boss, she was starting to lose feeling in her fingers and toes.

She probably wouldn't have agreed to join Maura outside today, except it was her first day at her new programming job and she didn't want to start off with her boss thinking she wasn't a team player. After all, it wasn't as if she had any assignments to work on yet. She had spent most of the morning filling out new-hire paperwork, and Maura had only just finished giving her a tour of the DataRightly offices before claiming she needed a short break.

"You don't have to stand here with me," Maura said, squinting at Kat. "You're obviously cold."

'Cold' was an understatement, but Kat didn't want to admit as much. "I'm okay," she said instead.

Maura looked around, her brow furrowed. "I wonder where Sadie is today."

"Who's Sadie?" Kat asked.

"Sadie Cramer. She's another hopeless nicotine addict, the only other one working in this building as far as I know. We made a pact to quit together once, but you know how that goes."

Kat smiled, trying to keep her teeth from chattering. "At least you're trying."

"Not hard enough." Maura's face lit up. "Oh, look at that."

Maura jabbed her cigarette toward the side of the building. When Kat saw what had caught her attention, she jolted. The fluffy white face of a cat was barely visible above one of the snowbanks.

"He looks as cold as you do," Maura told Kat.

"Have you seen him before?"

Maura shook her head. "First time ever."

Kat wondered whether the cat belonged to someone or if he was a stray. His body was hidden behind the snowbank, making it difficult for her to tell what kind of physical condition he was in.

But her lack of knowledge about his health didn't prevent her from worrying about him. As cold as it was now, the temperature would drop even more after the sun went down. This was no weather for a cat to be outside in.

"I should see if he'll let me get close to him," Kat said.

"What will you do if you catch him?"

"Call Imogene Little. She'll either know how to find his family or she can take him into 4F custody."

"What's 4F?"

"Furry Friends Foster Families. It's a nonprofit organization, and Imogene and I are both board members. Our mission is to help homeless animals find permanent homes and place them with foster families in the interim."

"Hey." Maura set her free hand on Kat's arm. "You're the group who took in Leo's cat after he died, aren't you?"

Kat nodded, feeling a pinch in her chest. She still remembered the shock she had felt upon hearing about Leo Price's murder—a murder that had occurred in the very parking lot they were standing beside.

"How's he doing?" Maura said. "Leo's cat, I mean."

"Right now Stumpy is being cared for by the Belleroses, one of our foster families."

Maura's lips twitched. "His name is Stumpy?"

"Yes, on account of him being a Manx and only having a little stump for a tail."

A pained look swept across Maura's face. "I bet he misses Leo. I know I do. I'm still getting used to not seeing him around DataRightly anymore."

Maura's words weighed down Kat's heart. "I'm sorry I didn't know him better."

"Oh, you would have gotten along great. It was hard not to like Leo." Maura rolled her cigarette between her fingers. "I should look into adopting Stumpy, for Leo's sake. I've been thinking about getting a pet for a while now anyway. It gets lonely living all by yourself."

Kat grinned, thinking of her own cats and how they made her laugh every day. "Well, I, for one, can attest that having a cat or two at home really makes the days brighter. And from what I've heard, Stumpy is a very friendly cat, once he gets to know you and comes out of his shell."

Maura smiled. "I knew I made a good choice hiring you. You have a heart as well as a brain. I could tell when I interviewed you."

"Oh." Kat flushed, unsure how to respond to the praise.

"Where do you think he came from?" Maura said, jerking her chin toward the white cat.

Kat shifted her attention back to the feline hiding behind the snowbank. "I'd have to guess from one of the houses down there," she said, pointing.

"His owner probably let him out, and he

wandered over this way."

"Or he snuck out, got lost, and doesn't know how to get home."

"Go see if you can catch him," Maura urged. "Maybe he's wearing a collar that will tell you where he lives."

Kat started toward the white cat, moving slowly so as not to alarm him. He watched her, but otherwise didn't seem bothered by her approach.

"Hi there, kitty," she crooned. "What are you doing out here all by yourself?"

The cat stared at her as if he suspected she was only speaking to him because she'd lost her mind.

"So I talk to cats," she said. "What of it?"

His whiskers twitched.

"I have two of your kind at home, you know. Their names are Matty and Tom."

The white cat stretched his jaws into a yawn, clearly unimpressed.

"Are you going to let me pick you up?" Kat asked him.

He tilted his head as though seriously considering her offer. But when Kat bent down and extended her hand, he turned around and dashed off, disappearing behind the building.

Kat stood up and sighed. "So much for that."

She glanced over at Maura, who was watching her with an amused quirk to her lips. Kat lifted her hands up in defeat.

She was on her way back to rejoin her boss when something in the next snowbank caught her eye. She crept closer, spotting the edge of a purple glove. She reached down to pick it up, figuring she could leave it in the lobby in case someone had dropped it. But before she could grab it she saw something that froze her whole body.

This glove looked as though it were already covering someone's hand.

Goosebumps broke out over Kat's skin. She forced herself to peek over the wall of snow, which was when she saw there was indeed a hand inside the glove—and the hand was attached to a woman who looked almost as pale as the snow surrounding her.

CHAPTER TWO

Maura's scream echoed through the parking lot, nearly giving Kat a heart attack.

"That's Sadie!" Maura shouted. "Sadie Cramer!"

Kat twisted around, coming face-to-face with her boss. Maura must have snuck up behind her while Kat was still reeling from the shock of what she'd found.

Maura looked at Kat with huge eyes. "Is she dead?"

"I—I don't know." Kat crouched down and picked up the woman's gloved hand to check for a pulse.

"Oh my goodness, she's dead," Maura muttered, not bothering to wait to hear whether Kat discovered any signs of life. "She's dead. *Dead.* I can't believe Sadie's dead."

Kat set the woman's hand down, feeling as if a stone had settled in her chest. Unfortunately, she couldn't dispute Maura's statement.

"We have to call the police." Maura fumbled in her coat pockets with her cigarette-free hand. "Where's my phone? I must have left it on my desk."

"I have mine." Kat reached for her pants pocket before she remembered the new slacks she'd worn for her first day on the job didn't have any. "Actually, I don't. My cell is upstairs in my purse."

Maura pivoted around, her eyes wild, before she looked back at Sadie. "We'll use Sadie's phone."

Kat waited for her to retrieve it, but Maura stood rooted in place. Evidently she expected Kat to do the honors.

Kat swallowed. "Do you know where she keeps it?"

"Try her coat."

Kat held her breath as she extended her hand toward the woman's coat. Her stomach was roiling at the notion of pawing through a dead person's clothes, but she also wasn't sure she had the strength to run back upstairs for her own phone. Besides, it seemed wrong somehow to leave Sadie out here by herself.

Luckily, Sadie's iPhone was tucked inside the first pocket Kat checked. She withdrew it and turned it on.

"It's password protected," she said, her heart sinking.

"Use 1-1-2-4," Maura suggested.

Kat did, unable to hide her surprise when the combination worked.

"November 24 is her birthday," Maura said, her face crumpling. "She'd just turned sixty."

Kat dialed 9-1-1 with shaky fingers, forcing aside thoughts of how Sadie had only lived a handful of days past such a personal milestone.

"9-1-1, police, fire, or medical?"

Somehow, Kat managed to keep a clear enough head to answer all of the dispatcher's questions. When they ended the call, she cradled Sadie's phone in her palms, wondering whether she should put it back where she'd found it. But the thought of touching Sadie again, even if it was only her coat, seemed too intrusive. She slipped the phone in her own coat pocket instead.

"I can't believe she's dead," Maura muttered over and over again as she and Kat stood there waiting for the first responders to arrive.

Kat hugged herself, trying to get warm. It

felt twenty degrees colder now than it had ten minutes ago, although she suspected that had more to do with the discovery of Sadie's body than any change in ambient temperature.

"What do you think happened to her?" Maura asked.

"I have no idea."

Maura's eyes drifted toward Sadie's body. The smoldering cigarette in her hand was all but forgotten. "She was in excellent health. She did yoga and all that. And her daughter's a nurse, so I'm sure she knows all the warning signs for heart attacks and strokes and whatnot. Sure, she smoked, but that wouldn't cause somebody to keel over."

Kat swallowed past the tightness in her throat. If Sadie hadn't died from natural causes, there were only a few options left—options that made Kat's veins feel as if they were filled with ice water.

"You should go inside," Maura said, clearly misinterpreting the cause of Kat's shiver.

"The dispatcher said to wait here."

"We can wait inside just as easily." Maura glanced at the cigarette in her hand, as though she were surprised to see she still had it. She stubbed it out on the sidewalk and tossed the butt into the garbage can near the door.

"C'mon."

Maura grabbed Kat's arm and steered her into the building. Warm air swirled around them when they stepped through the doors. But as chilly as Kat had been outside, the change in temperature didn't offer her any relief. Instead, the artificially hot air felt smothering, and she had to work to draw it into her lungs.

"Let's sit over here," Maura said, dragging Kat over to a bench by one of the floor-to-ceiling windows that flanked the entrance.

"Tell me about Sadie," Kat said when they were both situated.

"She's a career counselor." Maura pointed down the corridor. "Her office is at the end of the hall."

Kat peered down the corridor. Although she thought of the building as the DataRightly building, the software company only occupied the second floor. A dozen or so other small businesses leased space on the ground level.

"How long have you known her?" Kat asked.

"About a year, since she moved her business into this building." Maura flashed Kat a sad smile. "I kept telling her we should do something together after work, something besides smoking, but we never did. I guess I figured we'd always have more time."

An ache bloomed in Kat's chest. "There's just no telling when somebody's time will be up."

"I guess not."

A car pulled into the parking lot, causing them both to sit up straighter. But Kat deflated when she saw it was just an ordinary vehicle.

She and Maura watched in silence as a tall blonde swung her legs out of the car. She wore oversized sunglasses and kept her shoulders hunched as she hurried toward the building. When she stepped inside, she paused.

"Maura?" she asked.

Maura offered her a weak smile. "Hi, Rachel."

Rachel took off the sunglasses and slipped them into her purse. "Are you okay? You look really pale."

Maura scooted closer to Kat and patted the bench beside her. "You might want to sit down for this."

"Sit down for what?" Rachel asked.

"Sadie's dead."

Rachel's jaw slipped open, her eyes widening as she grasped the gravity of Maura's words. After standing there in stunned silence for a long moment, she finally stumbled over to the bench and practically collapsed onto it.

"Are you s—sure?" Rachel stammered.

Maura nodded. "Kat here checked for a pulse."

Rachel peered at Kat as though to evaluate how likely she was to have mistaken a living woman for a dead one.

"Were you here to see her?" Maura asked Rachel.

"I came to pick up my last paycheck."

Maura nodded, then turned to Kat. "Rachel used to work for Sadie," she explained. "She was her receptionist."

Rachel sucked in a breath. "Oh gosh."

"What?" Maura said. "What is it?"

Rachel's eyes were so wide that Kat could see the whites around them. "How did Sadie die?"

"We don't know yet," Maura said.

Rachel pulled her hands into her lap and wrung her fingers together. "She was too fit to have dropped dead. She had to have been murdered."

Maura gasped. "Murdered?"

Kat cleared her throat, causing both women to whip toward her. "We don't know for sure that Sadie was killed. She could have fallen down. Maybe she slipped on the snow and hit her head."

"That seems more likely than a murder," Maura agreed.

"Right. As of this moment there's zero evidence that somebody deliberately killed Sadie." Kat wasn't sure whether she was trying harder to convince them or herself. "And there's no sense in speculating until the responders get here. They can tell us what really happened."

Rachel didn't appear to hear her. "I hope the police don't think I killed her." She grabbed Maura's arm. "Do you think they'll arrest me?"

"Of course not," Maura said. "Why would you think that?"

"Because Sadie let me go. They might think I hated her for that. They might think I snapped." Rachel's knuckles turned white around Maura's arm. "This isn't going to look good for me, especially after Allen."

"Allen?" Kat asked.

"Allen Bolt. He's the lawyer with the office next to Sadie's. I worked for him up until a few months ago." Rachel folded her arms across her chest. "And before you go thinking I messed up, I didn't. He had money problems and couldn't afford to keep me any longer."

"Cherry Hills is so small it has to be tough for a business owner to make a go of it here," Maura sympathized.

"Yeah," Rachel agreed. "He does all these wills and trusts for rich people, but I guess that doesn't translate into much of an income." She sighed. "Bummer for me."

"I'm sure you'll find work soon." Maura patted Rachel's knee. "Sadie always told me your talents were wasted as a receptionist anyway."

Rachel's eyes filled with tears. "Oh, Maura. How can she be gone?"

The atmosphere grew heavy and, except for the occasional sniffle emitted by Maura and Rachel, the lobby fell silent. Sitting so close to them, Kat couldn't help but absorb some of their grief as her own.

It wasn't until she heard the distant sound of approaching sirens that Kat felt as if she could breathe again.

CHAPTER THREE

"She was murdered, wasn't she?" Kat said to Andrew Milhone.

"That's going to be for the coroner to determine," Andrew replied.

"But you're here," she pointed out. "Why would they call a police detective to the scene if Sadie had died accidentally?"

Andrew pushed his sandy blond hair away from his eyes. "Going back to when you found Sadie Cramer, what prompted you to notice her in the snowbank?"

Kat pursed her lips. She didn't like how he had dismissed her question, but neither could she really fault him for wanting to take back control of this conversation. After all, Andrew was here on behalf of the Cherry Hills Police

Department, not because he was her boyfriend. She couldn't expect him to give her the inside scoop just because they were dating.

"Kat?" Andrew said. "I asked what caused you to notice Sadie outside."

"I heard you." She thought about his question. "There was a cat." Her pulse accelerated at the memory. She had forgotten all about the runaway cat after the shock of finding Sadie.

"A cat?" Andrew said.

"A white cat. He was sitting next to Sadie, but he took off before I could catch him." Kat crossed the building lobby and peered out the window. "I don't see him now." She looked at Andrew. "Did any of your fellow officers notice him?"

Andrew lifted one shoulder. "None of them mentioned seeing a cat."

Kat wasn't surprised. Not only did a white cat blend in seamlessly with the snow, but the authorities had been called here to handle a dead person. She doubted they would give a cat a second glance even if they did happen to spot him.

"I hope he's okay," Kat murmured.

"You can look for him as soon as we release the scene," Andrew said.

"When will that be?"

"Sometime before the workday ends." He smiled at her then, his dimples melting her heart. "You look good in your professional gear, by the way."

Kat glanced down at her new outfit, unable to derive much joy from Andrew's compliment. Standing in the downstairs lobby giving her boyfriend an official police statement was not how she had envisioned her first day at Data-Rightly unfolding.

Andrew tapped his pen against the notepad. "So, do you have anything else to add?"

Kat shook her head. "I'll call you if I think of anything later."

"Do that." His eyes twinkled. "Or call me later regardless."

She grinned. "I just might do that."

Andrew surveyed the lobby. "Now if you'll excuse me, I need to take a few more statements."

"See you later."

Andrew walked over to Maura, who was standing on the other side of the lobby. Even from this distance Kat could see Maura's hands shaking. She wondered if her boss was still upset about seeing her friend's body outside or if she were simply feeling the effects of having left half of her cigarette unsmoked.

Kat decided to wait for Maura before heading back upstairs. Not only was there nothing for her to do until Maura showed her what to work on, but she wasn't in the mood to field any questions from her coworkers about what was going on outside. By now they had to have heard the sirens and seen the flashing lights of the emergency vehicles gathered in the parking lot.

She really just wanted to go home. But of course that wasn't an option. What would Maura think about her leaving early on her first day, before she'd had a chance to do much more than fill out some personnel forms?

Besides, Kat couldn't leave yet, not before she made more of an effort to hunt down the white cat.

She stepped closer to the glass and scanned the parking lot, unsurprised when she failed to spot the cat. With all the activity outside he had undoubtedly sauntered off in search of a more quiet place to brave the cold. Either that or he had blended in with the snow again.

Kat was still staring out the window when she felt a tap on her shoulder. She turned around to see Maura standing behind her.

"How was the interview?" Kat asked.

"Okay," Maura replied, but her face was still

too pale and her hands continued to tremble. "Detective Milhone is talking to Rachel now."

Kat wondered if Rachel would share with Andrew what she'd told them about Sadie firing her recently. Probably, she guessed. Something that easy for the police to verify would be silly to hide.

"I came over to tell you you can take off if you want," Maura said.

"Now?" Kat looked around for a clock but didn't see one. "It's not even noon yet, is it?"

"I don't know, but I don't have the energy to go back upstairs." As if to prove her point, Maura slumped onto the bench they'd occupied earlier. "I don't even think I have the strength to drive home."

Kat felt a flicker of concern. "Would you like me to call somebody for you?"

Maura shook her head. "I should be okay. I just need to sit here for a while. But you can go."

Kat didn't move, reluctant to let Maura out of her sight. She looked as if she might pass out.

Maura glanced up, straightening when she saw Kat staring at her. "Well, go on then," she said, her tone more firm. "I won't think badly of you, if that's what you're worried about. Nobody would expect you to be able to concentrate on programming after this. Come in an hour early tomorrow if you want, and I'll go over your first assignment then."

Kat nodded, knowing there was no point in staying if Maura wasn't going to show her what to work on. "I'll just run up and grab my things then."

Maura bobbed her head in acknowledgment before her shoulders drooped, her body seeming to cave in on itself.

Kat kept one eye on Maura as she inched toward the elevator. She took some comfort from the fact that Andrew wasn't too far away. If Maura did end up fainting, he would help her.

Upstairs, Kat grabbed her purse and mittens without being stopped by any of her coworkers. They probably hadn't even noticed her return. Most of them stood in clusters by the windows lining the front of the building as they watched the activity outside.

Clearly she wasn't the only DataRightly employee whose productivity was approaching zero for the day.

She took the elevator back downstairs. As soon as she ducked outside the cold air blasted her in the face. She stopped to pull on her mittens, listening as the breeze carried over snippets of the conversation happening several yards away.

". . . blunt force trauma . . ."

". . . unlikely that gash was caused from a fall . . ."

". . . bashed the side of her skull . . ."

". . . homicide . . ."

Kat shivered. She didn't need to hear any more. Although she had already suspected foul play thanks to Andrew's presence on the scene, what she'd heard confirmed it.

Sadie Cramer had been murdered.

She was still dwelling on that when she became aware of a faint rustling behind her.

She spun around. No one was there, but the rustling continued. It seemed to be coming from the garbage can next to the building entrance.

Kat considered ignoring it, not wanting to confront a rat. But a familiar furry white head popped over the rim of the receptacle before she could walk away.

"White cat!" Kat was thrilled to see him, and not just because he wasn't a rodent. "I've been worried about you."

His tail swished, giving Kat hope that he remembered her from earlier too.

"Are you homeless?" she asked. "I can help you if you are."

But her word clearly wasn't enough to convince the cat. When she moved forward, he scooted backward. His hind feet slipped on the edge, and he tumbled into the can.

Kat peered over the side, watching as the cat scrambled around in a panic. Her heart went out to him, but she didn't dare try to grab him. As frightened as he was, he would probably lash out.

After a frantic couple of seconds, the cat pulled himself back onto the rim of the can. This time he didn't bother to stick around for more conversation. As soon as he found his footing, he vaulted onto the ground and bolted around the side of the building.

Kat sighed, helpless to do anything but watch him.

She was waiting to see if he would reappear when the sun reflected off of something inside the garbage can. She leaned closer. Something shiny was half nestled underneath a discarded fast food wrapper.

She moved the wrapper aside, exposing what looked to be a stapler. The stapler was tipped sideways, a brownish sauce marring its metal surface.

A cold dread settled in the marrow of Kat's bones as the implications of what she was looking at penetrated her brain. If the substance on the stapler was what she feared it was, there was a good chance she was looking at the last thing Sadie Cramer had ever seen, right before it was hurled at her head.

CHAPTER FOUR

"Boy, am I glad to see you guys," Kat said to her two cats, Matty and Tom, as she shut the door to her apartment unit.

Tom ambled over to her, meowing the whole way. Kat tossed her coat onto the couch to free her hands. When she stooped down to pet the brown-and-black cat, Tom flopped over and stretched his arms above his head so she would have easy access to his stomach.

Kat could feel the stress of the morning evaporating as she rubbed his tummy. "Is this all you think I'm good for, Tom?"

Matty jumped off the couch where she had been snoozing and came over to join them. She sat down about two feet away and curled her tail around her paws, patiently waiting for her turn.

"What do you say I open up a can of wet food for you and Tom?" Kat suggested to the yellow-and-brown tortoiseshell. "That ought to prove these hands of mine are good for something besides belly rubs."

Matty's green eyes lit up as if she actually understood Kat's words.

Kat showered the felines with a few more minutes of attention before proceeding to the kitchen. As soon as the cats saw where she was headed, they streaked after her, determined to be present for whatever she had planned next.

She opened a cabinet and pulled out a can of cat food. Before she even had a chance to hook her finger through the pull tab, Tom started meowing frantically and Matty began weaving between Kat's legs.

"Anybody watching would think you didn't have two bowls full of kibble over there," Kat said, spooning the wet food into two plastic dishes.

The cats peered up at her as if to ask how she could seriously think wet and dry food were comparable substances.

Kat finished dividing up the food. She had to be careful not to step on either feline during her trek to their feeding corner across the kitchen. Matty and Tom apparently thought she might run off with their lunch if they dared to leave her side.

The cats dove for the bowls the second they touched the floor. Kat shook her head as she watched them gobbling up the salmon morsels.

"I see you both are perfectly content to ignore me now that you have something more important to focus on," she said, setting her hands on her hips.

Matty lifted up her head long enough to shoot Kat a disdainful look. Then she promptly stuck her nose back into the dish.

The cats were almost done eating when a faint chirping sound echoed throughout the apartment. Tom's ears pricked, and his pupils dilated. Matty swiveled toward the living room, her eyes gleaming.

Kat groaned. "Don't tell me a cricket got in here."

The chirping continued. Tom scuttled out of the kitchen in full stealth hunter mode. Matty, who had less of a flair for the dramatic, simply trotted after him.

Tom headed straight for the sofa. He pressed his nose against the edge of Kat's coat, then reached up and gave the fabric a pat.

"It's in my coat?" Kat wondered if she could toss the garment out the window and retrieve it in the morning, after the cricket had had ample time to wander off on its own.

Matty pounced on the coat, her tail swishing back and forth as her eyes darted around to see if she'd stirred anything loose.

The cricket stopped chirping. Kat wasn't sure whether that made her feel better or worse. Matty could have squished it.

The cats didn't move for several seconds, on alert as they waited for their prey to reveal itself again. When enough time had elapsed for Kat to start thinking about searching the coat herself, the chirping started again.

Tom's whiskers twitched. He reached his paw out again, batting at one of the pockets. An iPhone tumbled onto the carpet. Its face was lit up, and the chirping doubled in volume.

Kat laughed. "So it wasn't a cricket after all, just a ringtone."

She walked over and scooped the iPhone off the floor. She had forgotten she had it or she would have handed it over to the police earlier.

She glanced at the screen, her stomach clenching when she saw the words 'Son—Home' lit up. Was this Sadie's son calling for his mother? That could only mean he hadn't yet heard about Sadie's fate.

Kat stared at the phone, debating over

whether or not to answer. On the one hand, Sadie's son had a right to know about his mother's demise. On the other hand, he shouldn't hear the news from a complete stranger.

Before she could decide what to do, the phone stopped chirping. She exhaled, glad the choice had been taken out of her hands.

But before she could relax too much, the chirping started up once again. Clearly Sadie's son wasn't going to give up.

Kat steeled herself and punched the button to connect the call. "Hello?"

"Sadie, it's about time you picked up," an angry female voice said.

"Actu—"

"Barry told me what you did," the woman continued, talking over Kat. "How could you? How could you cut Barry out of your will like that?"

Kat's mouth gaped open, the accusation rendering her speechless.

"He's your own flesh and blood!" the woman went on. "He's as much your son as Ginger is your daughter. Did he do something to annoy you? If that's the case, you talk to him! You don't have your will redone!"

"Um," Kat tried again. "This—"

"I'm sure Barry feels the same way, although

he would never say so. 'It's Mother's money, she can do what she wants with it,' is what he'd say. But the money isn't the point, is it? It's the statement you made by cutting him off, like you'd disowned him. That's really hurtful."

Kat cleared her throat. "Um, this isn't Sadie."

"What?" the woman spat.

"This isn't Sadie. I just have her phone."

There was a brief silence before the woman came back on the line, her angry tone now replaced by one of confusion. "Who is this?"

"My name is Kat Harper."

"Kat Harper? Are you a friend of my mother-in-law's?"

"No, not really. I didn't know her."

"Didn't know her?" A pregnant pause elapsed. "What do you mean, *didn't*?" Clearly she hadn't missed Kat's use of the past tense.

Kat closed her eyes. "Look, this probably isn't my place to tell you—"

"Good grief. She's dead, isn't she?" the woman blurted out.

"I'm sorry."

"This is unthinkable." There was no trace of rancor left in the woman's tone now. She sounded choked up, and Kat could hear her gasping for air. "Barry. How am I going to tell

Barry?"

"The police haven't contacted him yet?"

"Police?" the woman screeched. "Why would they tell us anything?"

"I just figured . . ." Kat trailed off, not wanting to explain that Sadie had been murdered. "Anyway, I'm sorry for your loss."

"I can't believe Ginger didn't tell Barry," the woman said. "Ginger knows, doesn't she?"

"I'm not sure."

"She must. She's Sadie's golden child, the one she turns to for everything."

Kat didn't miss the bitter edge to the woman's voice as she said the last part. "I take it you're Sadie's daughter-in-law?"

"Chloe Cramer," the woman said. "I married her son Barry. Her disinherited son, I should say."

"Do you mind letting Barry know about his mother?"

"Sure." Chloe paused, then said, "Sorry to have bothered you."

Kat was about to assure her it was okay, but Chloe had already disconnected the call.

Kat placed Sadie's iPhone on the coffee table and sank into the sofa. Her mind was reeling.

Could Barry have killed his mother because she'd cut him out of her will? Kat wondered. If he shared Chloe's angst over being disinherited, he was certainly a viable suspect.

Or what about Barry's sister Ginger, the woman Chloe claimed to be Sadie's sole heir? Had Ginger decided she couldn't wait to get her hands on her inheritance once she found out everything was being left to her? Possibly, although Chloe had called her Sadie's golden child. Would a golden child murder her own mother?

Or, maybe Chloe herself was guilty. She'd certainly sounded angry enough to do the deed. Except she'd just phoned Sadie to chew her out. She wouldn't have done that unless she thought Sadie was still alive.

A terse meow interrupted Kat's thoughts. Matty sat on her right, and Tom was perched on her left. Both cats were staring at her with feline dismay.

It was only then that Kat realized she was sitting on her coat—the exact same coat the cats believed to still be harboring a cricket.

"The cricket isn't real," she told them.

Neither cat budged. Knowing they wouldn't be satisfied until they had a chance to investigate firsthand, Kat stood up.

Matty didn't waste any time resuming the hunt. As soon as Kat was out of the way, the tortoiseshell buried her head under the coat. Spotting movement from the cricket's last known hiding spot, Tom pounced, and pretty soon the cricket was all but forgotten as the cats started playing with each other.

Their antics would have sent Kat into a fit of laughter under normal circumstances, but at the moment her mind was elsewhere. She couldn't stop playing through her conversation with Chloe, knowing it would haunt her until Sadie's killer was caught.

CHAPTER FIVE

Kat pulled into the DataRightly parking lot at seven o'clock the next morning. A few lights were on, but the building as a whole was still dark. She had expected as much, considering that the official start of the workday didn't begin for another hour.

Thoughts of Sadie Cramer had kept her from sleeping well. After talking to Chloe she had called Andrew and told him about having Sadie's cell phone. He had promised to stop by sometime today to pick it up.

Unable to resist scrolling through the iPhone's call history, she had been startled to note that Sadie's last call had been to Bob Bellerose, one of 4F's foster parents and Stumpy's current caretaker. The timestamp indicated that

Sadie had phoned him shortly after ten yesterday morning. Maura and Kat had gone outside around eleven, which meant Bob might be one of the last people to have talked to Sadie before her death.

Maura's interest in Leo's cat struck Kat as the perfect opening for her to get in touch with Bob. She would call him later and set up a time to bring her boss by to meet Stumpy. While they were there, she could casually ask if he knew who Sadie might have run into after she'd talked to him.

Kat got out of her car, her eyes veering toward the snowbank where she had found Sadie's body. She wondered if the white cat was lurking nearby. She had brought him some of Matty and Tom's kibble, placing it in a plastic lid fished out of the recycle bin. She didn't plan to feed him every day, but neither could she let him starve out here in the cold.

She brushed aside some snow near one corner of the building and set the food down. Meanwhile, she couldn't stop herself from searching for evidence that Sadie's killer might have left behind. Although the authorities had already combed through the area, with all this snow they could have easily missed something.

Kat didn't unearth anything, but that didn't

prevent her from running through possible scenarios as she headed for the building entrance. After her phone conversation with Chloe yesterday, she certainly had enough suspects to keep her mind occupied.

Or maybe Sadie hadn't known her killer. Perhaps she had caught a car thief by surprise when she'd come out for her smoke break. Maybe he'd just happened to have a stapler handy and used it to keep Sadie from telling anyone what she'd seen.

Kat was so lost in her own head she almost plowed right into the man standing by the building entrance.

"Oh, gosh," she stammered, stopping short of jabbing him with her key.

The man's own key ring tumbled to the ground. Kat hurried to pick it up for him, but in her rush she grabbed it too hard and ended up depressing one of the buttons on the car fob. A black sedan beeped and flashed its lights.

Kat dropped the keys into the man's hand before she could do anything else to embarrass herself. "Sorry."

He smiled at her. "No problem." He aimed the fob at the car and pressed another button to quiet it. "You're lucky this thingamajig actually works. Three months ago I was driving an old rust heap that preferred to remain unlocked rather than obey any commands I gave it."

His joking manner caused Kat to relax. At least he didn't seem too upset with her.

He tilted his head. "You looked like you had a lot on your mind."

"I do."

"Care to share?"

Kat pulled at one of her mittens. "Oh, I was just thinking about the woman who was killed here yesterday."

The man grimaced. "Sadie Cramer."

"Did you know her?"

"I know most of the people who work in this building." He squinted at Kat. "But I don't recognize you."

"I just started at DataRightly yesterday."

"That explains it then." He held out one gloved hand. "I'm Allen, Allen Bolt. I rent one of the first-floor suites."

"Kat Harper." She shook his hand. He had a strong, firm grip. "You're a lawyer, right?"

He grinned. "Guilty as charged."

"I met your receptionist yesterday," Kat told him. "Rachel. Or, rather, I gather she's your former receptionist."

He frowned. "Rachel was here yesterday?"

"She came to pick up her last paycheck from

Sadie."

"Huh. I didn't see her."

"She stopped by after the police were already on their way," Kat informed him. "I don't think they let her get past the lobby."

"Well, that explains why she didn't pop in to say hi."

"Did Rachel get along well with Sadie?"

"Yes." Allen fiddled with his keys. "Although . . ."

"Although . . . ?"

"Nothing." He shook his head. "I shouldn't have even brought it up."

Kat studied him, itching to know what he had been about to say. Had he witnessed Sadie and Rachel fighting on occasion? Perhaps Rachel had a temper that only a former employer would know about.

Not wanting to drop the subject, Kat said, "Rachel told me Sadie hired her after you let her go."

Allen bobbed his head. "That's correct."

"That was nice of her. I'm sure Rachel appreciated it."

"Sadie was like that. Always willing to help a person out, ethical to almost a fault."

"Ethical to a fault?" Kat repeated.

Allen flicked his wrist. "All I meant is that

saving Rachel wasn't Sadie's job."

"You're saying she shouldn't have hired her?" Kat asked.

"Oh, Rachel is a good worker. I would have kept her on myself if I could have afforded her." Allen held up an index finger. "Now, I know what you're thinking. Attorneys should have oodles of money, enough to sleep on mattresses stuffed full of hundred-dollar bills when they finally stop billing for the day."

Kat feigned surprise. "You don't?"

"Unfortunately we all can't be one of those celebrity lawyers you see on television. After all, there are only so many ex-NFL players and burnt-out singers to represent." Allen laughed. "But, then again, I didn't choose the path of a high-profile criminal attorney either. I'm in estate planning, one of our profession's more boring branches."

Kat smiled. "Sounds about as interesting as computer programming."

"Ah, but do you enjoy it? That's the real question."

"I do." Kat slipped her key in the lock and pushed the door open. She could see no point in continuing this conversation out in the cold.

Allen pulled off his gloves as he followed her inside. "And I enjoy my work as well. There's nothing more satisfying than knowing you've helped to get someone's affairs in order. Tell me, do you have a will?"

Kat blinked. "I'm sorry?"

"I was inquiring as to whether you have a will."

"Um, no."

"You ought to think about writing one," Allen advised. "I'd be happy to help you draft it."

Kat was only thirty-two. She had nothing that was worth much. And, except for Matty and Tom, she had no dependents. A will seemed superfluous.

"It's never too soon to plan for the inevitable," Allen said, as if he could read her mind. "Wills, trusts, power of attorney, I can help you with any of it. I'll tell you right now, you'll sleep better once you get all that done."

Kat ignored the sales speech, too focused on a possibility that had just entered her mind. "You didn't happen to do Sadie Cramer's will, did you?"

"Why yes, I did. Why do you ask?"

"I was curious whether it led to any strife within her family."

Allen tapped his chin. "Well, I can tell you, there's nothing that gets relatives up in a knot more than dividing up somebody's possessions after they're gone. Part of it, I'm sure, is the stress that comes from losing somebody. That often stirs up a lot of unresolved feelings, and those feelings come out in the oddest of ways."

Kat frowned. She didn't miss how he had avoided giving her a direct answer. Although, what had she really expected from a lawyer?

Allen checked his watch. "I should get going. I've got a full day's work ahead of me."

"It was nice meeting you," Kat said.

"You too, Kat."

She watched as he disappeared down the hall, wondering what insights into Sadie's family he had just taken with him.

CHAPTER SIX

"I can't tell you how glad I am to be out of the office," Maura told Kat, one hand on the steering wheel while the other held a lit cigarette. "When I'm there I keep gravitating toward the window, wondering if I could have prevented Sadie's death if only I had bothered to look outside yesterday morning."

Kat's heart went out to her boss. "What happened to Sadie isn't your fault."

"I know, but still." Maura wedged her cigarette in her mouth as if to cut herself off from saying anything more.

Judging from the car's overflowing ashtray and the easy way Maura kept one elbow propped on the driver's side door as she flicked ashes out the window, Kat gathered she was used to driving while smoking. In fact, the more time Kat spent with her boss outside of the office, the more she was starting to view Maura's cigarette as a natural extension of her hand.

At least she'd had the courtesy to crack the windows, Kat mused. Even so, her throat was starting to feel scratchy.

Maura glanced at the dashboard clock. "The Belleroses said they'll be home by noon, right?"

"Yes. I only talked to Bob, but he said Meg will likely be there too. He thinks she'll do a better job explaining Stumpy's quirks so you know what you're in for before you make a decision about adopting him."

Maura smiled. "It'll be good to see them."

Kat regarded her across the console. "You know the Belleroses?"

"Yes, but I didn't know they were doing this cat fostering thing." Maura took another drag from her cigarette. "Actually, Bob's father has been in and out of the hospital where Sadie's daughter works. She's a nurse there. Sadie used to rave about how good she was with all her patients."

"Oh." Sometimes Kat forgot how everyone in Cherry Hills seemed to be connected in some way.

Maura sighed. "I still can't believe Sadie's

gone. Who am I going to smoke with now?" Her eyes flitted in Kat's direction. "I mean, you're always welcome to join me."

"I appreciate that, but I know it's not the same." Inhaling Maura's secondhand smoke wasn't something Kat planned to turn into a regular activity.

"Here we are," Maura said, pulling into the Belleroses' driveway.

Kat slipped off her seat belt. She had been to the Belleroses' place before. Bob and Meg had been fostering for 4F longer than Kat had been on the board.

"I'm excited to meet Leo's cat," Maura said, stubbing out her cigarette in the car ashtray. The motion sent a few other butts tumbling onto the floorboard, but Maura didn't seem to notice. "It's been years since I've had a pet of my own."

Kat couldn't prevent the smile that spread across her face when she recalled how Matty and Tom had spent all of yesterday afternoon searching the apartment for their 'cricket.' "They're a lot of fun."

They climbed out of the car and headed up the driveway. Kat kept her arms close to her sides to contain her body heat. As grateful as she was to be breathing in fresh air again, she wished it wasn't so cold.

The door swung open seconds after Maura depressed the doorbell, revealing an older gentleman with a potbelly and a welcoming smile. "Maura O'Malley," Bob Bellerose said, spreading his arms. "You're looking gorgeous, as always."

"Hi, Bob." Maura gave him a hug. "How's the heart?"

"Still beating." He grinned at Kat. "Afternoon, Kat. I almost didn't recognize you without Imogene by your side."

"I gave her the day off," Kat joked.

Bob chuckled. "And here I thought you two came as a pair. Truth be told, I believe Imogene views you as one of her stray animals."

"Oh." Kat didn't know how to respond to that. She had never been compared to a stray animal before.

Bob stepped aside. "Well, come on in, ladies. Meg's in the living room."

Kat followed Maura into the house. Bob shut the door behind them before veering toward an armchair and picking up a magazine. Now that they had been let in, he apparently thought his duty as host was finished.

"Maura, Kat," Meg Bellerose said. She stood up from the sofa, her chestnut-colored hair tumbling around her shoulders.

"Hi, Meg." Maura hugged her, then surveyed the room. "So, where's Leo's cat?"

"Stumpy is hiding under the coffee table," Meg said, pointing. "He's been sulking there ever since I dragged him out from under the bed and shut the bedroom door."

"Oh, look at that precious little darling," Maura cooed, rushing toward the gray cat. "Isn't he just the cutest thing you've ever seen?"

Stumpy, evidently, wasn't nearly as enamored with Maura. As soon as she reached out to pet him, he bounced toward the opposite side of the room and hunkered down in the corner.

Maura didn't seemed perturbed by the rebuff. She laughed. "He runs like a jackrabbit."

"It's the effect of not having a tail," Meg said, grinning.

"Well, I think it's darling." Maura sat down on the couch, her eyes sparkling as she watched Stumpy's attempts to compact himself into an invisible ball.

"He's actually a very sweet cat," Meg said. "But he's also very shy. It takes him some time to open up to new people."

"I don't blame him. Nowadays it's hard to know who to trust." A shadow crossed over Maura's face. "There are a lot of evil people out there."

"You're referring to what happened to Sadie Cramer, I presume," Meg said.

Maura nodded, her face grim.

"I heard about it at the hospital," Bob piped up, lifting his head from his magazine. "I knew something was wrong when her daughter didn't show up for her shift yesterday. Found out later from one of Pop's nurses what had happened."

"Bob's father has cancer," Meg said. "Unfortunately, it's terminal."

Kat felt a pinch in her chest as she took a seat next to Maura. "I'm sorry."

"Well, we knew when he was diagnosed a year ago that his chances of beating this thing weren't high," Bob said, setting down his magazine. "Pop went through all the treatments they suggested, but they couldn't get rid of everything. Nothing to do now but wait."

Meg walked across the room and perched on the ottoman in front of Bob's armchair. She gave him a watery smile as she set her palm on his knee.

Bob patted her hand. "But, Pop's eighty-seven. He's lived a full life, a good life. I only wish he hadn't had to suffer so much this past year." He shrugged. "At least I convinced him to get a trust set up when he was first diagnosed.

Now he can go without worrying about leaving any loose ends behind."

Bob's words reminded Kat of what Allen Bolt had said that morning. At the time she'd figured all that talk about a will giving her peace of mind was just a ploy to drum up more business, but maybe there was some truth to it. Maybe there was a certain comfort in knowing your last wishes were well documented.

Unless, of course, your last wishes ended up being the cause of your death, Kat thought, thinking of Chloe railing about Sadie's will.

Meg smiled up at Bob. "I take comfort in the fact that when your father's time comes he'll be surrounded by people who love him."

Bob squeezed her hand. "In some ways we're lucky we know Pop's end is near. Poor Ginger must be heartbroken she didn't get a chance to say goodbye to her own mother."

Kat decided now was a good time to bring up her other motive for wanting to see the Belleroses. "Bob, you didn't happen to talk to Sadie before she died, did you?"

Bob clucked his tongue. "You know, she called me when I was visiting with Pop yesterday."

"She did?" Meg said.

"Yes. I had forgotten all about it."

"What did she say?" Kat asked.

"She left a voicemail. Said she had something important to discuss and she wanted to do it in person." Bob frowned. "She didn't tell me what it concerned."

Kat processed that. Sadie's reluctance to discuss the matter over the phone made Kat think it was serious. Could it have also been what had gotten her killed?

"Look," Maura said. "He's decided to join us."

Stumpy had evidently grown tired of cowering in the corner. He was currently tiptoeing across the carpet, his gaze darting between Maura and Kat, the two strangers in the room.

Maura slid onto the carpet and held her hand out to him. "Think he'll come to me?"

"He might," Meg said. "If there's one thing I've learned about cats after all of my years fostering, it's that they don't like to be too predictable."

Stumpy did come, although he moved at the speed of a snail. When he finally made it to Maura, he sniffed each one of her fingers, looking ready to take off again if any of them failed to meet his approval. But Maura must have passed the test because soon he closed his eyes and pressed his head into her palm.

Everyone in the room let out a collective breath.

"Isn't he the sweetest thing," Maura whispered, almost reverently.

"He likes you," Meg said. "Give him another half hour and he might even sit in your lap."

"Unfortunately, we don't have that long," Maura said, checking her watch. "Kat and I should be getting back to the office soon."

Meg stood up. "I'll walk you out. Let me know what you decide about Stumpy, okay? Or come see him again when you have more time. Once he learns to trust you I think you'll discover he has a delightful temperament. And if you do end up adopting him, I'm positive you won't regret it."

"I'll definitely think about it," Maura promised, but Kat could tell from the huge smile on her face that her mind was already made up.

CHAPTER SEVEN

"Hey, look who's here," Maura said as she pulled into the parking lot outside the DataRightly building.

Kat peered out the windshield but didn't see anyone. "Who?"

"It's that white cat." Maura turned off the engine and pointed. "Over there."

Kat saw him then. He was hunched over the kibble she had left out this morning.

"He's wolfing down that food like he hasn't eaten in weeks," Maura commented, taking off her seat belt.

Kat recalled the zest with which Matty and Tom had devoured their wet food yesterday. Although she knew the white cat's own appetite didn't necessarily mean this was the first meal he'd eaten in a while, his enthusiasm wasn't easing any of her fears about him being out here on his own.

Maura reached for her door handle. "You want to try to catch him again?"

Kat climbed out of the passenger seat. "You don't mind? You were going to show me that section of code that's been giving you headaches."

"That can wait." Maura looked at her watch. "Besides, we've still got twenty minutes left on our lunch break."

"I'll see you upstairs in fifteen," Kat promised.

"Take your time." Maura waved as she ducked into the building.

The sound of the door opening and closing prompted the white cat to lift his head. His gaze locked with Kat's, but he seemed more curious than scared.

"Hi there," Kat said, moving closer. "Remember me?"

He licked his paw and used it to scrub one side of his face.

"I left that food for you," Kat told him. "I have two of your kind at home, and the thought of you out here without anything to eat really bothered me."

The cat set his paw back on the ground, his tail sweeping across the snow.

"Do you have food where you live?" Kat asked.

The feline stared at her.

Kat sighed. "I wish you could talk."

He meowed.

Kat couldn't help but laugh. "Oh, so you *can* talk. My mistake."

Kat held her breath as she inched closer. When she made it within a few feet of her target, she held out her hand but didn't touch him. He eyed her fingers warily.

"May I pet you?" Kat asked.

She stretched her arm out a little farther and brushed her fingers against his fur. He didn't seem to mind, but neither did he do anything to encourage the contact.

Kat stroked him a few more times. She was just starting to feel optimistic about picking him up when a car pulled into one of the short-term parking slots a few yards away. The cat's head jerked up, and he spun around and dashed off.

Kat huffed, disappointment washing over her. "So much for that."

Andrew got out of the car. His face lit up when he spotted her. "What are you doing out here?"

Kat walked over to him. "I was trying to catch that white cat."

"He's out here again?"

"Not anymore. But he did eat some of the food I left for him."

"Well, if you're feeding him, he's sure to come back."

"What about you?" she asked. "What are you doing here?"

He grinned. "I came to see you."

Kat's heart skipped a beat. His dimples had that effect on her.

"You said you have Sadie Cramer's cell phone," he reminded her.

"Oh, right." Kat mentally chastised herself for thinking he had stopped by for a social call when he was in the middle of a case. "Here." She handed him the iPhone in her coat pocket.

"Thanks."

"The password is 1-1-2-4."

Andrew raised his eyebrows. "You know her password?"

"Maura knew it. Apparently Sadie wasn't shy about keeping it a secret."

Andrew frowned, and Kat could practically see what he was thinking. Someone as prudent as Andrew wouldn't think highly of giving out personal information such as passwords.

"What about the stapler?" Kat asked. "Were you able to get any fingerprints off of it?"

"Nothing usable."

Kat tried not to let Andrew's words get her down. "Well, assuming it was used to kill Sadie, it kind of suggests her killer didn't come here yesterday with the intent to harm."

"What makes you say that?"

"If somebody drove over here intending to commit murder, he or she would have chosen a more conventional weapon, don't you think? I know if I were planning to get rid of somebody, a stapler wouldn't be the first item I would think to bring with me. But if I were already here and saw an opportunity, well, it might be one of the more convenient things to grab."

Andrew rubbed his chin. "Your logic makes sense."

Kat squinted at him. She didn't miss how she was the only one throwing theories out there. "Do you know where that stapler came from?"

Andrew averted his eyes. "Possibly."

She set her hands on her hips. "Care to share?"

Andrew dragged his gaze back to hers. "Kat, you know I can't discuss an active investigation."

Kat wasn't surprised by his response, but it still stung. Sometimes she had a difficult time coming to terms with the fact that her boyfriend had the type of career that prohibited him from being as open about what he was working on as she wanted him to be.

But Andrew's refusal to discuss the case details didn't stop her from speculating.

Kat eyed the DataRightly building. If Andrew had already pinpointed where that stapler had come from, it had most likely been Sadie's. That meant her murderer had to have been inside her office recently. Maybe one of her clients had been on the receiving end of what they thought was some bad career advice. They could have swiped her stapler on the way out, then hidden outside until she emerged for her smoke break.

Kat's thoughts shifted to Rachel. She would have had just as much access to that stapler as a client. Perhaps she hadn't really stopped by yesterday to pick up her paycheck after all. Maybe she'd come here to exact revenge on the woman who had fired her. But then why would Rachel have returned with that paycheck story after the deed was done?

Unless she'd realized later she had left something behind that could implicate her, Kat thought, her heart beating faster. She could have returned to retrieve the evidence only to be intercepted by Maura and Kat before she had a chance to sneak back into Sadie's office.

Kat spun toward Andrew. "Have you searched Sadie's office yet?"

Andrew reared back. "Excuse me?"

"Have you searched through Sadie's office for clues her killer might have left behind?"

Andrew peered at her down the bridge of his nose. "Kat, you do realize I know how to do my job, right?"

Kat folded her hands in front of her. "Of course."

"Good."

They stared at each other for a silent moment. Kat was about to apologize for questioning his competency when he coughed.

"I should get going," he said. He bent closer and gave her a kiss. The kiss was neither quick nor chaste, which told Kat he had already forgiven her. "See you later."

She watched him climb into his car, the heat of his kiss spreading all the way to her toes. Seeing Andrew—even if he was frustratingly mum when it came to discussing his cases—always put her in a better mood.

CHAPTER EIGHT

After Andrew left, Kat searched briefly for the white cat, but he was long gone.

Trying not to feel too dejected, she went inside the DataRightly building. While she waited for the elevator, she glanced down the corridor.

The hallway was empty. From here she could see the doors leading to the different businesses on this floor were all made of glass. How long would it take her to walk to the end and peek into Sadie Cramer's office? She could just take a quick look around in search of missing staplers or something obvious that Rachel might have left behind, then come right back to the lobby. It would be a two-minute detour, tops.

Before she could fully contemplate what she was doing, her feet started moving of their own volition. The pull of Sadie's office was almost irresistible.

She glanced at the businesses she passed as she hurried down the hall. She spotted a few people through the glass doors, but they didn't pay her any heed. They were all busy with other things.

A doorplate sporting Sadie's name over the words CAREER COUNSELOR was affixed next to the last office on the left. Cupping her hands around her face, Kat peered through the glass door. On the other side she could see a reception desk and a small waiting area. Behind the desk, Sadie's inner office was partially visible through an open door. A second door on the other side of the desk was closed. Kat guessed that it led to a bathroom, kitchenette, or some combination of the two.

Movement drew Kat's attention back to the reception desk. She nearly fell over when she realized someone was sitting there.

Kat didn't move, her brain struggling to work out who she was looking at. Sadie was dead. Rachel no longer worked for her, and as far as Kat knew she hadn't hired another receptionist.

So who was the fortyish brunette sitting behind the desk?

Deciding there was only one way to find out, Kat tested the doorknob. It turned without resistance.

The brunette looked up. "We're closed," she said, peering at Kat over the top of her reading glasses.

"That was the impression I was under," Kat replied, stepping inside. "I'm Kat Harper. I'm the one who found Sadie outside yesterday."

The brunette shot up off the chair, her hands flying to her mouth. "You're the person who found Mama?"

"Mama?" Kat repeated.

The woman tossed her reading glasses on the desk and circled around to Kat's side. From this distance, Kat could see the dark circles under the woman's bloodshot eyes. She looked as though she hadn't had a good night's sleep in days.

"I'm Ginger Cramer," the woman said. "Or, I should say Hamilton. That's my married name."

"Oh. I didn't realize you worked for Sadie."

"I don't." Ginger wrung her hands together. "I'm here to see Allen Bolt, actually."

"Allen Bolt?" Kat echoed. "You mean the estate lawyer?"

"He works in the office over there," Ginger said, jerking her chin toward the door. "When I arrived half an hour ago there wasn't anyone in his waiting room and I heard voices coming from his private office. I figured he was with another client and decided to wait over here."

Kat looked out the glass door, her eyes landing on Allen Bolt's door across the corridor. Ginger's story made sense. From Sadie's reception desk she would have a clear view of anyone entering and exiting the office across the hall.

Ginger walked over to one of the two visitor chairs and sat down. "It feels strange being here without Mama. It's too quiet."

Kat lowered herself into the empty chair next to Ginger. "How did you get in?"

"Mama gave me a key a long time ago, when she first opened up shop here." Ginger paused, then said, "What did she look like when you found her?"

Kat stiffened, the question taking her aback.

"Did she look like she was at peace?" Ginger asked, tears filling her eyes. "Did she look like she went painlessly?"

"I—I don't know." Kat didn't care to mention the bloody stapler she'd found in the garbage.

Ginger slumped in her seat. "I hope Mama

didn't feel anything. I'm a nurse, so all I see all day are sick people. People who are dying. People in pain." Tears fell from her eyes and dripped down her cheeks. "I couldn't stand knowing Mama died in agony."

Ginger buried her face in her hands and wept. Kat's heart squeezed in sympathy. She wished now she had kept her mouth shut about finding Sadie. Better yet, she shouldn't have entered Sadie's office at all. She should have just looked through the door then left as originally planned.

Reminded of her motive for venturing this way, Kat surveyed the reception desk. She spotted a hole punch, a cup full of pens, and a paper clip dispenser, but no stapler. Neither did she see anything that suggested Rachel might have been here recently, although she wasn't exactly sure what she was looking for in that regard.

Ginger pulled a tissue out of her pants pocket and dried her face. "Mama was the one who encouraged me to go into nursing. She wasn't officially a career counselor back then, but she's always had a knack for it. She said she always knew I was meant to be a caregiver."

"Speaking of that, I talked to the son of one of your patients yesterday," Kat said.

"You did?"

"Bob Bellerose. I take it his father doesn't have much longer."

Ginger folded and unfolded the tissue in her hands. "Yeah. Right now we're just trying to keep him comfortable. At some point we'll recommend hospice care."

"Bob said Sadie called him yesterday to tell him something, something she didn't want to talk about over the phone. Do you know what that was about?"

Ginger stopped playing with the tissue and stared at Kat. "I have no idea."

"She didn't mention whatever it was to you?"

"No." Ginger's forehead wrinkled. "But she wouldn't have called Bob just to chat. They weren't friends."

"But they obviously knew each other," Kat said.

"This is Cherry Hills," Ginger replied, the implication being that most people in town knew one another.

That was true enough, Kat supposed. "When was the last time you talked to Sadie?" she asked.

"This past weekend, Thanksgiving. My husband and I went over to Mama's house for dinner. But Mama didn't say anything to me about the Belleroses. And she seemed too cheery to have anything important on her mind."

Kat didn't know how much to read into that. Whatever Sadie had wanted to talk to Bob about could have been something she'd only discovered yesterday, might not have concerned her family, or the topic simply could have been one she didn't want to discuss over Thanksgiving dinner.

Ginger sagged in her seat. "I guess there's no chance of finding out what Mama wanted to say now."

"I guess not," Kat said, although she couldn't help but wonder if it related to her death.

Ginger tossed her tissue into a nearby trash can, then looked around the office. "I suppose I should make arrangements to close up her business. Mama operated a one-woman shop here."

"Did she ever talk about Rachel?" Kat asked.

"Her receptionist?" Ginger nodded. "But Mama only hired her to be nice. She couldn't stand the idea of her not having a job so close to the holidays. It was never supposed to be permanent."

"Yet she fired her before Thanksgiving," Kat

mused.

"Yes, but not before she gave Rachel several leads on where she could find work. One of them was a friend of hers who manages a toy shop. She always needs extra help over the holidays."

"Oh." Kat hadn't realized Sadie had gone to the effort of finding Rachel another job before letting her go.

Ginger crossed her legs. "Mama offered Rachel free career advice while she was working for her, you know. She said Rachel had a lot of potential, if only she would apply herself. Honestly, Mama thought Rachel was rather lazy. Smart but lazy, was what she told me. She thought Rachel just hadn't found a job she was passionate about yet."

"Were most of your mother's clients happy with the advice she gave them?" Kat asked.

"Sure." Ginger squinted at her. "Why do you ask?"

Kat fidgeted, not wanting to admit she was attempting to fish out potential murder suspects. "Oh, I was just thinking."

A sound from the corridor saved Kat from having to explain further. A man walked out of Allen Bolt's office and disappeared down the hall.

Ginger scrambled out of her seat. "Well, I should go talk to Mr. Bolt." Her face crumpled. "Mama's estate is one more thing I have to take care of now that she's gone."

Kat stood up. "I heard she's leaving you everything."

Ginger stilled. "Where did you hear that?"

"From your sister-in-law."

Ginger scowled. "Chloe, the big blabbermouth. I don't know what Barry sees in her."

"Chloe sounded pretty upset that your mother didn't leave them anything."

"Yeah, well, she's not even a blood relative."

"According to her, Barry feels the same way."

"Shows what she knows." Ginger scoffed. "Barry's the one who encouraged Mama to change her will."

Kat rocked backward. "He is?"

Ginger walked over to the desk and dug through her purse until she found a compact. She opened it and held the mirror up to her face. "I took care of our father when he was dying," she said, scrubbing at the tear streaks on her cheeks. "He was sick for a couple years."

"I'm sorry," Kat said.

Ginger started powdering her nose. "Honestly, him finally passing on was the best thing that could have happened. It was torture watching him suffer. Barry couldn't stand it either. He did everything he could to avoid seeing Dad toward the end."

Kat could commiserate. She didn't think she would handle that type of situation very well either. It made her admire Ginger's chosen career all the more.

Ginger snapped her compact shut and stuffed it back in her purse. "After Dad passed I think Barry started feeling guilty about not being there very much. He told Mama that since I was the one who had cared for Dad, I should be the one to get what he and Mama left behind. Mama resisted for a long time. She didn't want Barry to think changing her will meant she valued him less, even though he was the one encouraging her to do so."

"But she finally agreed," Kat said.

"She had it done last week, as sort of her sixtieth birthday present to us, I guess." Tears filled Ginger's eyes again. "Just in the nick of time."

Kat's heart grew heavy. She didn't say anything as Ginger started sobbing again, her grief washing away the makeup she had only just reapplied.

CHAPTER NINE

Kat was grateful when five o'clock finally rolled around. Although it had been a bit of a thrill to be looking at code again, she was ready to go home and crash. Her brain had been on overload all day, Sadie's murder vying with Kat's new job for attention.

Kat rested her head against the back of the elevator as it descended. When the doors opened to let her out on the first floor, Allen Bolt was emerging from the hallway.

"Looks like we're on the same schedule today," he said, halting beside her.

Kat adjusted her purse strap. "I guess so."

"I don't know about you, but this time of year I always feel like I'm going home in the middle of the night. What happened to our long summer days?"

Kat glanced outside. "At least it's not snowing."

Allen smiled. "Ah, you're an optimist."

Kat regarded him. So far she had asked both Bob Bellerose and Ginger about the phone call Sadie had made to Bob yesterday, but she had yet to ask Allen. Given that they worked next door to each other and Sadie had made that phone call during business hours, it was conceivable she might have mentioned what it was about to Allen.

It wouldn't hurt to ask, anyway.

"Allen," she said, "did Sadie say anything to you yesterday about something being on her mind?"

"Something on her mind?" he said.

"I don't have any specifics, but she called Bob Bellerose less than an hour before she died. Apparently she had something important to tell him, but she didn't want to do it over the phone."

Allen rubbed his chin. "Now that you mention it, she did make a comment to me."

Kat's pulse quickened. "What did she say?"

"She—" Allen abruptly stopped talking. His eyes darted around before he tipped his head toward Kat and lowered his voice. "I would prefer if we don't talk about it out here. Do you mind if we discuss this in my office?"

"Not at all." There was no way she was leaving before she heard what he had to say.

She followed him down the hallway. As exhausted as she had been a minute ago, now her brain was buzzing. What did Allen have to tell her?

She supposed she would find out soon enough.

Kat waited as patiently as she could while Allen sifted through his key ring. When he finally located the right key and unlocked the door, it was all she could do not to plow over him in her haste to get inside so she could hear what he had to say.

In terms of layout and furnishings, his office was an exact replica of Sadie's. He locked up behind them and headed for the inner office. "Come on in," he said.

Kat followed him inside and sat down, setting her purse in her lap. Allen's office was a mess. Folders were spread all over the desk and on top of the long file cabinet lining the wall. Haphazardly stacked legal pads practically obscured the desk blotter. And in the center of it all sat a computer monitor lined with at least a dozen sticky notes.

Allen closed the door and shrugged out of his coat. "Please forgive the disarray. I wasn't expecting anyone else to be in here until tomorrow afternoon."

"No problem. So, about Sadie."

Allen paused from hanging his coat on a wall hook. "You don't beat around the bush, do you?"

"My curiosity is getting the better of me," Kat admitted.

"I understand." He hung up his coat and eased into the leather chair behind the desk. "Before I say anything, I must be clear that whatever I tell you stays between us."

"But if it could help identify who killed Sadie—"

"Then I suppose I have an obligation to go to the police," Allen said, finishing her thought. "But for our purposes, I must ask you to be discreet. Although she didn't tell me this while I was acting as her lawyer, Sadie was nonetheless a client. That means I am bound by certain expectations of confidentiality."

"Oh," Kat said, seeing his dilemma. "In that case, I'll be sure not to say anything."

Allen smiled and started straightening some folders. "I'm glad we understand each other."

Kat scooted her chair forward. "So, what is

it that Sadie told you?"

Allen folded his arms on the desk. "You know Hank Bellerose is sick, correct?"

"If that's Bob's father, then yes. I heard he has cancer."

"He does." Allen looked past her shoulder, a grave expression on his face.

Kat glanced behind her, but other than a few diplomas on the walls and a window that overlooked the parking lot, there wasn't much there.

"Sadie came to me with a problem about her daughter," Allen finally continued.

"Ginger?"

He nodded. "She works at the hospital. Sadie had some . . . concerns about what she was doing there."

"What was Ginger doing?"

"I didn't really understand the specifics. I'm not a medical professional."

"Neither was Sadie," Kat pointed out.

"No, but she had a better grasp of hospital procedure than I do. That was something she must have picked up from Ginger."

"Okay," Kat said, anxious to hear where he was going with this.

"Sadie said Ginger was . . ."

"She was . . . ?" Kat prompted.

Allen sighed. "She was taking items from the

hospital that should have been going to her patients."

"Items? You mean medications?"

"Yes. And I gather some of these medications were slated to be received by Hank Bellerose."

Kat recalled Ginger's emotional breakdown in Sadie's office. At the time she had assumed Ginger was grieving, but what if her reaction had really been borne out of guilt? Ginger had to realize if knowledge of what she was doing got out she could not only lose her job but be prosecuted. What if she'd chosen to kill her own mother rather than risk Sadie exposing her secret?

The possibility gave Kat chills.

"How did Sadie find out what Ginger was up to?" Kat asked.

"She didn't share that with me."

"Did you tell the police all this?"

Allen shook his head. "The whole conversation slipped my mind until you asked about it just now."

"You have to tell them," Kat said, sticking her hand in her purse. "Let me call Andrew—I mean, Detective Milhone."

Allen's eyes widened. "Now? It's after five. He must be off duty."

"Trust me, he'll want to hear this."

Kat found her cell phone. But before she had time to hit the speed dial for Andrew, Allen sprang out of his chair and swiped the phone from her hands. His abrupt motion not only sent the phone tumbling to the floor, but several folders slid off the desk as well, papers scattering everywhere.

Kat jumped up from her seat, knocking her purse over in the process. "What are you doing?"

"My apologies," Allen said, sinking back into his chair. "You just took me by surprise, is all."

"*I* took *you* by surprise?" she said, placing one hand over her racing heart. "I think you've got that backward."

"Kat, I'm going to level with you." Allen set his palms flat on the desk. "I'm not ready to talk to the police yet."

"Why not?"

"I don't want to betray Sadie's confidence. Talking to you after you agreed to keep this conversation a secret is one thing. But once the authorities are involved, word will get around. People will start to believe I'm the type of lawyer who doesn't think twice about breaking client confidentiality."

"But if what Sadie told you could help nab

her killer, I'm sure she'd want you to share it," Kat argued. "Don't you have a moral obligation to say something?"

"I have a moral obligation to keep my clients' business between us."

"Sadie is dead. She's way beyond caring about her secrets getting out."

He stared at her for a long moment, then nodded. "Perhaps you're right. I'll contact the authorities tomorrow, after I've worked out how to tell them without violating attorney-client privilege."

Kat didn't figure there was much use arguing. She could tell from the tilt of Allen's chin that he wasn't going to budge.

But she could be as stubborn as anyone else. "You'll call Detective Milhone first thing in the morning?" she said, unwilling to leave until he promised.

"Yes."

"I'll give you his number."

She scanned the mess on the floor in search of her cell phone, finally spotting it poking out from under one side of Allen's desk. As she knelt down to retrieve it, her eyes landed on a check lying atop a pile of disturbed papers. The check was for the amount of two thousand dollars, written out to Allen Bolt. But what really caught her attention was the account associated with the payment: Bellerose Trust.

The hairs on the back of Kat's neck prickled. She thought again of Sadie's phone call to Bob Bellerose. The check was dated yesterday. Assuming it had been written out in the morning, Sadie could have noticed it while wandering over to chat with her neighbor. Could this be what she had wanted to talk to Bob about? But why would Sadie feel the need to report to Bob how much Allen charged his clients?

Unless this money wasn't compensation for Allen's services, Kat considered. Was this check actually proof that he was stealing from the Bellerose Trust? And had Sadie somehow figured out what he was doing?

Given that she had ended up murdered, that was a very real possibility. She could have been killed to make sure she never had the opportunity to tell Bob Bellerose what his father's estate planning lawyer was up to.

The room seemed to tilt as the check blurred in front her. Kat squeezed her cell phone like a lifeline, struggling to understand the implications of what she was looking at.

"Find your phone?"

Allen's voice nearly caused Kat to bang her

head into the underside of the desk. She scrambled upright.

"Got it," she said, holding up the phone as if to prove she hadn't been lingering on the floor for another reason.

Allen relaxed into his chair. "Good."

Kat stared down at the desk, unwilling to look Allen in the eyes in case he could see her suspicions. Her heart was pounding so hard she could feel it in her temples. She needed to get out of there.

She drew in a breath. "Well, I should get going."

"You haven't given me that detective's number yet," Allen reminded her.

"Oh, right."

Kat lifted her phone closer to her face, but her fingers were trembling so badly she dropped it again.

A hand wrapped itself around her bicep, causing her to yelp. Allen had circled around the desk and grabbed her.

"You looked a little unsteady there," he said.

She fought against him.

Allen let go and held his palms in the air. "Hey, calm down."

"Don't touch me," she said.

"What's your problem?" he snapped. "I was

helping you."

He started to reach for her phone, but his arm froze in midair. Kat could tell the exact moment he spotted the check. His face reddened, and when his head jerked back up his nostrils were flared.

His reaction all but solidified her suspicions.

Kat backed away from him. "You killed her," she said, the words tumbling past her lips before she even knew she was going to say them.

CHAPTER TEN

Time seemed to stop as Allen stared at her. Kat couldn't breathe. All she could do was wait to hear what he would say.

After what felt like an eternity, Allen's shoulders slumped. "I had to," he said, three simple words that were as good as a confession.

Kat ran her tongue around her parched mouth. "So all that stuff about Ginger . . ."

"It was a lie," Allen said. "I made that up to throw you off my trail. But now that you've seen the check, there's no point in pretending." He gestured toward the chair Kat had vacated. "Sit down, and I'll tell you everything."

Kat didn't move. The last thing she wanted to do was sit down. She felt like a trapped animal inside this office. Sitting would only increase her sense of being caged.

What she really wanted to do was make a run for it. But what were the odds she would be able to escape? Allen was bigger and stronger than she was. He could tackle her easily. And it was now after regular business hours. She could see through the window that only a few cars were left in the parking lot. With Allen occupying a corner office, the chances of someone hearing a cry for help were slim to none.

"Sit," Allen said again.

This time Kat obeyed, realizing she didn't have much choice. Besides, as terrified as she was, a part of her wanted to hear what he had to say.

Something on the floor caught her eye as she settled into the chair. Her breath hitched, but she quickly composed herself, hopefully before Allen noticed.

"Okay," she said, wrenching her gaze back to his. "I'm sitting, Mr. Bolt. Or do you prefer Allen?"

He eyed her funny. "Allen's fine."

He lowered himself into his own chair, a fact that eased some of Kat's discomfort. At least now he would have to stand up first if he decided to grab her again.

"Sadie stopped by yesterday," Allen began.

"You mean she stopped by here, your office?" Kat interjected.

His eyes narrowed. "Where else would I be talking about?"

Kat shrugged. "This is a large building, what with DataRightly taking up the whole second floor."

"Why would we meet at DataRightly?"

"You tell me."

He stared at her for a moment, then dismissed her with a scoff. "Anyway, as I was saying, I'd recently helped Sadie revise her will, and she wanted to make sure she'd done everything she needed to. While she was here, she happened to see something she shouldn't have." He eyed Kat. "The same thing you saw."

Kat couldn't stop her eyes from drifting toward the check on the floor.

Allen reached down and picked it up. "Several of my clients named me as co-executor on the trusts I set up for them."

"At your urging?" Kat asked.

He lifted a shoulder, which Kat took as a yes.

"That must make it easy to withdraw money from their accounts whenever you need a little extra cash," Kat said. "And I take it Bob Bellerose's father is one of the clients you're stealing from."

"Hank Bellerose is an ideal target. His health has degenerated a lot since he came to me to get his financial affairs in order. He isn't in any position to notice his money disappearing."

Kat's heart clenched. How sad that someone would view a sick, elderly man's imminent death as an invitation to take advantage of him.

"Sadie saw this sitting on my desk when she was over here yesterday," Allen said, rippling the check in the air. "I hadn't thought to hide it. I wasn't expecting anybody. She had popped over between clients."

"What did she say when she saw it?" Kat asked.

"Nothing. She merely started asking all these questions about trusts, things like how much I charge in maintenance fees and what the going rate is to set one up."

Kat could picture the scene, Allen blithely explaining his standard rates all the while Sadie grew increasingly suspicious as she attempted to fit what he was saying in with the two-thousand-dollar payment she'd spotted.

"At one point during our conversation I caught her staring at this," Allen continued, laying the check on his desk. "That's when her motive for asking all those questions hit me. She was fishing for an explanation as to why I was paying myself so much from the Bellerose trust."

"Except you had no explanation," Kat said.

"I tried to backtrack, to explain that at times I have to charge extra for certain services, but I could tell she wasn't buying it."

Kat swallowed. "So you killed her."

"I couldn't let her talk to the Belleroses. I knew she had a connection to them, through her daughter's employment at the hospital. All she would have to do is mention what she'd seen and they would start nosing around. They might even bring in the authorities. And once that happened, I would be toast. The truth would come out and my business would be destroyed."

Kat folded her arms across her chest. "As it should be."

Allen ignored the chastisement. "She left my office before I could stop her. But, lo and behold, about a minute later I saw her outside, talking on her cell phone."

Kat's gaze shifted to the window. From his corner office Allen had a clear view of the area near where Sadie had died. All he would have to do was look up from his desk.

"She must have left that voicemail for Bob Bellerose right after she talked to you," Kat guessed.

"I didn't know that until you told me. All I knew was as long as she was alive she would remain a threat. That look on her face when she left my office was a dead giveaway she wouldn't keep quiet about that check for long."

"That's what you meant when you said she was ethical to a fault."

Allen grimaced. "I didn't mean to say that. It slipped."

"Was that Sadie's stapler you used to kill her?"

He raised his eyebrows. "You know about that?"

"I found it in the garbage outside."

"Yes, it was Sadie's stapler. I took it from her reception desk. She always left her office unlocked during the workday, even when she went out. She was careless like that."

Kat thought about Maura knowing Sadie's iPhone passcode. It stood to reason that a woman who didn't think twice about giving out her passwords wouldn't bother to lock up for a five-minute absence. Obviously Sadie had never considered that her trusting—or careless —nature might one day end up facilitating her death.

Allen turned to look out the window, his eyes glazing over as if he were watching yesterday's events unfold all over again. "She was off the phone by the time I caught up to her. You should have seen the look on her face when she saw me. She started backing away, but there was nowhere for her to go."

His words made Kat sick to her stomach. Sadie had to have been terrified when she saw the man she had just caught stealing from a client cornering her outside with a stapler gripped in his hand.

"It was easier than I expected," Allen said. "And I wore my winter gloves, of course. I didn't want to leave my fingerprints anywhere."

Kat felt a flash of anger. "Didn't it bother you, killing a woman like that?"

Allen leaned back, looking startled by her accusation. "I did what I had to do."

"Is that how you justify stealing from your clients too?"

"The people I take from can afford to loan me some money."

"These aren't loans. You're taking money that isn't yours with no intention of paying it back."

"So what? You should see the fortunes some

of these people have. It's more money than any one person can spend in a lifetime."

Kat gripped the chair armrests and pulled herself closer to him. "But it's not yours."

His eyes hardened. "You don't know what it's like working for yourself. Six months ago I was drowning in debt. I even had to let Rachel go."

"What about your car?" Kat challenged. "The one I saw you drive up in yesterday. It looked new."

"It is new. But before I started on this side endeavor I was driving a junker that didn't start half the time. I was late to several meetings because of that old car. So, you see, I needed that money. I only took what I needed."

Kat could tell nothing she could say would suddenly make him develop a conscience. He had obviously already convinced himself he'd only done what he'd had to and was unwilling to listen to any reasoning to the contrary.

"I don't expect you to understand," Allen said, setting his elbows on the desk and steepling his fingers in front of him. "You get a paycheck from DataRightly every week. You don't need—"

Allen stopped talking, his forehead furrowing. Kat heard it then too, the sound of sirens approaching.

Seconds later, a police cruiser pulled into the parking lot, its lights flashing. Allen shot out of his seat and ran over to the window.

Kat stood up as well, but she didn't join Allen at the window. Instead, she bent over and picked up the object she had spied on the floor earlier.

Allen whipped around. "Did you call them?"

She held up her cell phone. "I must have accidentally connected the call to Detective Milhone when I was looking up his number."

"You mean he's been listening this whole time? He heard everything?"

Kat nodded.

Allen's hands balled into fists. "Why, you little sneak."

Kat's stomach lurched as Allen strode toward her. Although Andrew should be barging through the door any minute now, Allen still might be angry enough to try something before he got here.

Allen's head swiveled from side to side. Kat figured he was looking for something he could use to kill her like he had Sadie. The thought made her shudder.

Without waiting to see if he found anything, she pivoted around and lunged for the door. She yanked it open and raced through the reception area. On the other side of the glass door that exited into the corridor, she could see two uniformed officers and Andrew running in her direction.

"Get back here!" Allen shouted.

Kat hurled herself at the door. It didn't budge. She looked wildly around, her eyes coming to land on the lock. She flipped it back and threw the door open just before the police officers flew into the room.

"Police, don't move!" one of them yelled.

Allen froze, the color draining from his face. Kat didn't know if he actually thought he would have ample time to kill her and flee, but he had clearly intended to try.

Andrew jogged up to Kat and gripped her shoulders. "You okay?"

She nodded, too emotional to speak.

He guided her toward one of the waiting room chairs and pushed her into it. "Sit here."

She gulped down some air. "Did you hear everything?"

"I heard enough. As soon as I realized what was going on, I radioed for help." He grinned. "Smart thinking, feeding us clues about where you were without alerting Bolt that we were listening."

She collapsed against the chair. "You have no idea how much I wanted to give up pretenses and start screaming for you to get over here."

Andrew smoothed her hair back. "I'm here now."

And, Kat thought, for that she would be eternally grateful.

CHAPTER ELEVEN

"So, another case closed by Katherine Harper," Andrew said, flipping his notepad shut and tucking it back into his shirt pocket.

They were sitting on one of the benches inside the DataRightly building's first-floor lobby. Kat had just finished giving Andrew her statement. Allen Bolt had already been led away in handcuffs. She'd watched as the arresting officers drove off with him in the back seat, glad to see him in custody.

Now only she and Andrew remained on the premises. At least, they were the only humans on the premises.

She looked out the window. "I wonder if the white cat is still out there."

"I suppose we could go look for him," Andrew said.

"Now?" It was already dark outside, and Kat knew Andrew had to be as tired as she was.

"Why not? With Sadie's killer behind bars, there's nothing urgent on my plate. I can take an hour or so off before finishing up my paperwork."

Kat hooked her arm through his, her heart swelling. She knew he was only volunteering to look for the white cat because it was important to her. The fact that he was willing to sacrifice his evening for her made her appreciate how lucky she was to have him in her life.

"Okay," she said, jumping off the bench and heading for the door. "Let's go find us a cat."

Although it was colder now that the sun had gone down, being close to Andrew kept her body temperature elevated. If he would just agree to stick by her side whenever she ventured outdoors, she wouldn't need a new coat after all.

"I haven't yet had a chance to ask you how the new job is going," Andrew said, zipping up his jacket.

"You mean other than finding a dead body on my first day?" Kat asked.

He grimaced. "Yeah, other than that."

"I'm enjoying it, actually. I like my boss, Maura. She's going to adopt one of 4F's foster cats, you know."

"How'd you talk her into that?"

"I didn't have to. She volunteered."

"That's great."

"And it feels good to be getting back into programming," Kat went on. "I hadn't realized how much I'd missed it until Maura gave me this piece of code to work on."

Andrew smiled. "It's nice to see you this excited."

"I'll be even more excited if we can find that white cat."

"I've got a flashlight in my car," Andrew said.

Kat didn't argue, although the reflection of the parking lot lights against the snow still piled up alongside the building almost convinced her they didn't need a flashlight.

She looked around while Andrew fished in his trunk. She didn't see the white cat any-where, but she did note that the kibble she had set out earlier was now completely gone. The feline must have returned sometime this after-noon and gobbled up the rest of it.

Andrew held up the flashlight. "Got it."

"Let's start over there," Kat said, pointing.

"That's where he seems to hang out."

"Okay."

They walked over to the snowbank where she had first seen the cat. Being so close to where Sadie had died, she couldn't help but reflect on how drastically things could change in such a short period of time. It was hard to believe that less than thirty-six hours ago Sadie had still been alive. Now she was dead, destined to be sixty years old forever.

"Andrew, do you have a will?" Kat asked.

"No, why?"

"Just curious."

He stopped walking. "You're thinking about what happened back in Bolt's office, aren't you?"

Kat halted beside him. "You know, if I died —"

"Don't talk like that," Andrew cut in.

"You're a cop. Don't you ever think about your own mortality?"

His silence was as good as an answer in the affirmative.

Kat shoved her hands in her coat pockets. "Anyway, it's not like I own much. But Matty and Tom—"

"If, for some reason, you can no longer take care of them, I'll do it," Andrew said.

She met his gaze. "You will?"

"Sure. I love those cats."

A tingle raced up Kat's spine. Andrew still had yet to say he loved her, but somehow she couldn't imagine feeling any happier if she had been the subject of his declaration instead of her cats.

Andrew broke eye contact and shone the flashlight around, Kat's cue that he wanted to drop the subject of her death.

That was fine with her.

They didn't say anything as they scrutinized the landscape. It took a few minutes, but Kat finally spotted a tiny white face near the edge of the parking lot. "There he is," she told Andrew, excitement bubbling in her chest.

Andrew pointed the flashlight where Kat indicated, careful not to aim it directly at the feline. "Think he'll let you get near him?"

Kat thought about Stumpy working up the courage to trust Maura. "I hope so."

"I'll hang back here so I don't spook him," Andrew said, wandering off to the side. He only made it two steps before he stopped and redirected the flashlight beam at something wedged in a nearby snowbank.

"What is it?" Kat said.

"It looks like a piece of paper."

Kat squatted next to Andrew and started digging the paper out. It was damp after having been submerged in snow, and she had to be careful not to tear it.

Once she'd brushed enough snow aside to free the page, she brought it up to her face using both hands. Her heart lurched when she realized she was staring at a flier for a lost cat—a lost cat named Snowball who looked suspiciously similar to the one Kat had in her sights.

"Looks like he escaped over Thanksgiving weekend," Andrew said, leaning over her arm to read the flier himself.

"So he does have a home." The thought made Kat smile.

"Now we just have to get him there."

Kat handed the flier to Andrew. "You take this, and I'll see if I can grab Snowball."

Snowball hadn't moved from his spot across the parking lot. Kat started off in his direction, careful not to move too quickly. When she was close enough to touch him but not so close that he was likely to feel threatened, she crouched down and looked him in the eye.

"So now I know what to call you," she said. "Snowball."

Snowball's ears pricked as if he recognized his name. Maybe if she said it enough times he would start to understand she was on his side.

"Snowball fits you." She extended a hand toward him. "Are you going to let me pick you up, Snowball? I know you have a home, so you must be used to humans."

Snowball slowly closed his eyes before opening them equally slowly. Kat found the gesture encouraging. Maybe he would let her touch him.

She stretched her hand out a little farther and gave his cheek a light stroke. Snowball stood up and rubbed against her fingers. Kat petted him for a while before she dared to hook her hands around his chest. When he didn't offer any resistance, she lifted him up.

Andrew joined them, although he stayed a few feet back. "You got him."

"Yes." Kat could feel the steady thrum of the feline's body against her rib cage. "And he's purring."

"He only lives a couple blocks from here," Andrew said, reading off of the flier. He pointed. "That way."

Kat strode forward. "Then let's go."

Andrew fell into step beside her. "He's acting pretty docile. I'm surprised he's not fighting you more."

"He's probably had his adventure and is ready to go home."

And, Kat thought, hugging the cat close, she knew exactly how he felt.

NOTE FROM THE AUTHOR

Thank you for visiting Cherry Hills, home of Kat, Matty, and Tom! If you enjoyed their story, please consider leaving a book review on your favorite retailer and/or review site.

Keep reading for an excerpt from Book Eleven of the Cozy Cat Caper Mystery series, *Hit & Run in Cherry Hills*. Thank you!

Excerpt From

HIT & RUN
in CHERRY
HILLS

PAIGE SLEUTH

"Our January fundraiser is only six weeks away," Imogene Little said, her auburn ponytail swinging from side to side as she looked between the other two Furry Friends Foster Families board members. "So far the three of us have managed to secure five donations for the silent auction, but I think we can do better."

"I have a couple calls in to local business owners," Willow Wu said, pushing her dark hair away from her face. "And one of my fellow teachers knows the manager of a boutique clothing store. She thinks she can get her to donate a few items from last season's leftover inventory. She'll let me know next week."

"That's fabulous." Imogene rolled her chair

closer to her desk and made a note on the pad in front of her.

"Has anybody talked to Dorothy Fairchild?" Katherine Harper asked. "She gets all that promotional stuff for free, and she's always eager to support us."

Imogene scribbled on her pad. "That's a marvelous idea, Kat. Would you follow up with her?"

"Sure." Kat liked Dorothy Fairchild, or Lady Fairchild as she preferred to be called. She was positive the wealthy older woman would donate some swag without much encouragement.

Clover, Imogene's big white cat, sauntered into Imogene's home office. When he spotted Kat, he froze, one paw still in midair.

"Sorry for taking your armchair, but I needed a place to sit," Kat told the feline.

Imogene laughed. "You should have seen him earlier, when it was still daylight. A bird landed on the window ledge there, and he went nuts. He was climbing all over that chair, trying to figure out how to get to it through the glass."

Kat smiled at the image. "That sounds like something my cat Matty would do." She faced Clover and patted her thigh. "You're welcome to join me, kitty. There's enough room for both of us here."

Clover rotated his ears toward her as though considering her offer. Then he started moving again, leaping into Kat's lap with a force that knocked the air from her lungs. He tucked his paws under his chest and laid down, the soothing sound of purring filling the room.

Imogene tapped her pen against the desk. "Now, where were we? Any other places we can approach about donating items for our auction?"

"What about Fireside Gallery in Wenatchee?" Willow asked. "Several of their featured artists contributed small pieces the last time we organized one of these things."

Imogene bobbed her head. "And people are always more than willing to whip out the checkbook when local artwork is up for grabs."

"Why don't I stop by there this Saturday?" Kat volunteered. "I've been meaning to hit the Wenatchee malls for more work clothes anyway."

"I'll phone ahead so they know to expect you," Imogene said, making a note. "I should approach Nikita, too. She might donate something."

"Who's Nikita?" Kat asked.

"Nikita Stoll."

Kat waited for Imogene to elaborate, but

when no further explanation came she figured it was up to her to keep probing. "Who's Nikita Stoll?"

The pen fell out of Imogene's hand. "You don't know who Nikita Stoll is?"

Kat glanced at Willow, who looked equally stunned by what Kat had thought was a simple question. Her ignorance even appeared to shock Clover. He lifted his head and abruptly stopped purring.

"Sorry," Kat said. "Should I be familiar with this person?"

"She's only the most famous artist in Cherry Hills, maybe even all of Central Washington," Imogene said. "Her paintings have been displayed all over the country."

Kat shrugged. "I'm not really into art."

Clover stood up and jumped onto the floor, stalking away as though to put some distance between himself and someone so unworldly.

"You don't have to be into art to like Nikita's stuff," Willow said. "Her nature portraits are exquisite."

Imogene vaulted out of her chair with an agility more suitable for a woman half her age. "Let me show you one of her works."

Kat had no choice but to follow as Imogene grabbed her hand and dragged her out of the room. Imogene marched her through the living room like a drill sergeant before hauling her up the staircase.

Willow and Clover trailed after them, making Kat feel slightly claustrophobic. She hoped her shamefully poor eye for art wouldn't turn her into a laughingstock.

But, as it turned out, she needn't have worried. When they reached the master bedroom, the painting Imogene planted her under was so breathtaking that even Kat's lungs ceased working for a second. In the center of the canvas sat a beautiful lake surrounded by untainted wilderness. The water sparkled beneath a bright, yellow sun, the reflection of the eagle soaring in the sky visible between ripples. The level of detail was astounding, as though it were a high-quality photograph rather than something created by hand.

"Isn't it gorgeous?" Imogene said. "I get to stare at this every night before falling asleep."

"It's almost like being outside." Kat had the urge to reach out and touch the lake to see if her finger came away wet.

"And Nikita lives right next door. I'm practically bunking with a celebrity."

A clatter tore their attention away from the painting. On the other side of the room, Clover had hopped onto a chair and stuffed his upper body between the venetian blinds of a nearby window. Only his bottom half was visible as he stood on the toes of his hind feet, his tail swishing back and forth.

"Clover!" Imogene strode over to him. "What on earth are you doing?"

He pulled his head out of the slats and meowed.

Imogene grabbed hold of his torso. "You know you're not supposed to do that. You're going to ruin those blinds."

But Clover clearly didn't intend to leave his station. He used his hind legs to kick Imogene's hands away before releasing a long, drawn-out meow of displeasure.

Imogene opened her mouth as though to scold the cat, but before she could speak the squeal of tires sounded from somewhere outside. A split second later, a harrowing scream that ended as soon as it started could be heard through the window.

Imogene turned away from Clover, her mouth forming a perfect O. Kat's skin broke out in goosebumps as she, Imogene, and Willow exchanged wide-eyed glances. Then they all moved at the same time, falling into step one after another as they ran for the front door.

Excerpt from *Hit & Run in Cherry Hills*

* * *

Please check your favorite online retailer for availability.

ABOUT THE AUTHOR

Paige Sleuth is a pseudonym for mystery author Marla Bradeen. She plots murder during the day and fights for mattress space with her two rescue cats at night. When not attending to her cats' demands, she writes. She loves to hear from readers, and welcomes emails at: paige.sleuth@yahoo.com

If you'd like to join Paige's readers' group, please visit: http://hyperurl.co/readersgroup

Made in the USA
Lexington, KY
24 November 2016